ELF IN THE HOUSE

ELF IN THE HOUSE

Ammi-Joan Paquette

illustrated by Adam Record

SCHOLASTIC INC.

JINGLE –
JINGLE!

There's a girl in the house
on this snowy
Christmas Eve.

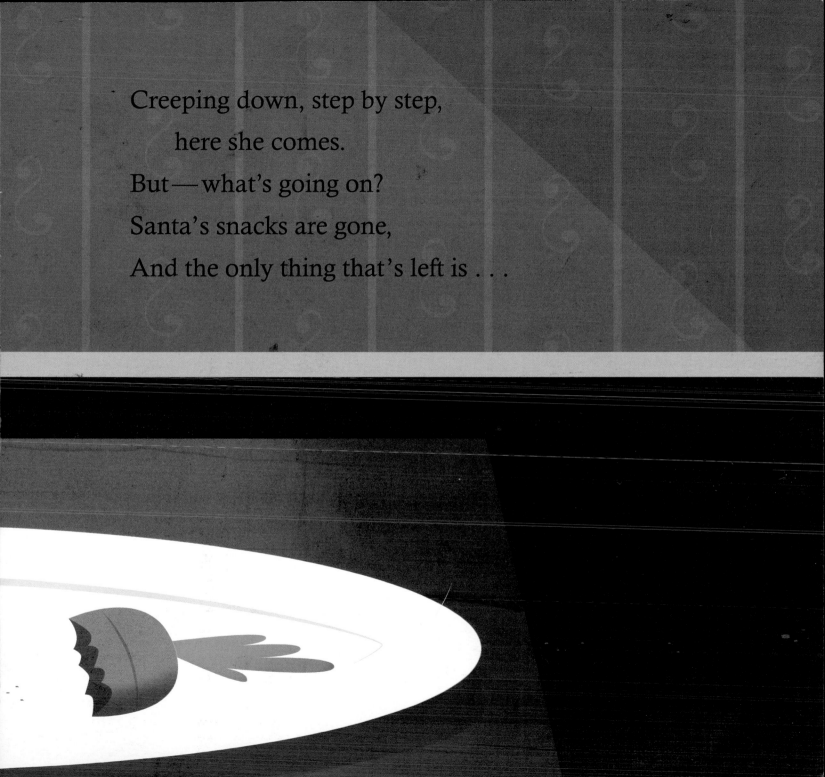

Creeping down, step by step,
  here she comes.
But—what's going on?
Santa's snacks are gone,
And the only thing that's left is . . .

CRUMBS!

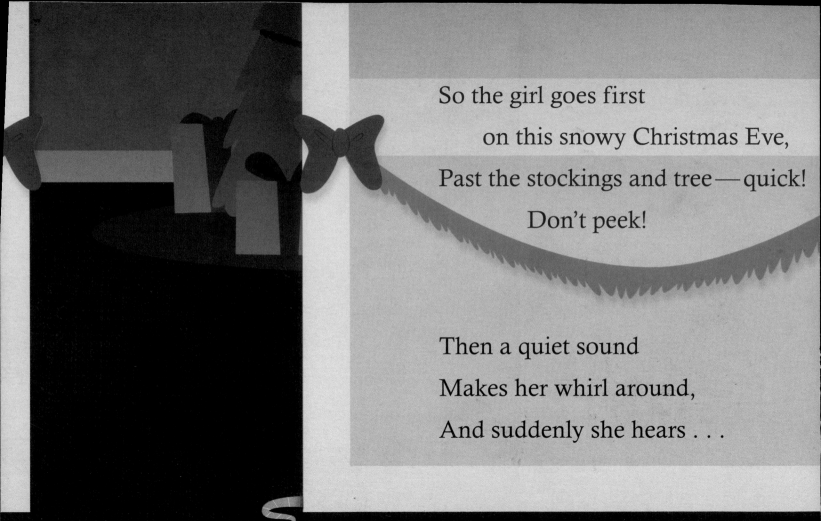

So the girl goes first
   on this snowy Christmas Eve,
Past the stockings and tree—quick!
   Don't peek!

Then a quiet sound
Makes her whirl around,
And suddenly she hears . . .

a SQUEAK!

And the MOUSE goes second
on this snowy Christmas Eve,
Marching on through the house with a wiggle.
Then a quick streak of red
Flashes by up ahead,
And suddenly they hear . . .

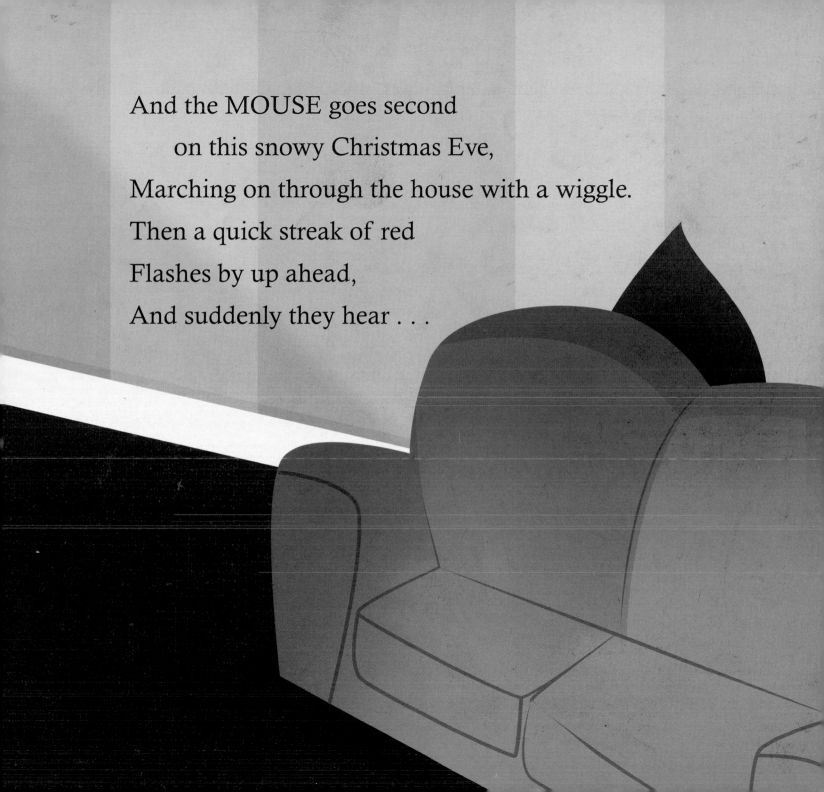

a GIGGLE!

And the ELF goes third
    on this snowy Christmas Eve,
In a line dance of jingle-bell hop!
Festive friends in a row,
Down the hall they go,
Until suddenly they hear . . .

CLIP - CLOP!

And the REINDEER goes fourth
   on this snowy Christmas Eve,
To a door topped with green mistletoe:
Season's joy gleaming bright
In a starburst of light,
And the *fifth* thing they hear? . . .

There's a party in the house
    on this jolly Christmas Eve,
Sharing treats as the night slips away.

It's the best time of year,
Filled with holiday cheer,

And tomorrow will be CHRISTMAS DAY!

For Kate Fletcher,
with my thanks, awe, and admiration
A. J. P.

For my wife and three amazing kids
A. R.

ISBN 978-1-338-32258-3

12 11 10 9 8 7 6 5 4 3 2 1   18 19 20 21 22 23

Printed in the U.S.A.   40

First Scholastic printing, November 2018

This book was typeset in Calisto MT and Sheree.
The illustrations were created digitally.